George E. Vickers

The Pharisee and Witch-Burner in Modern Politics

George E. Vickers

The Pharisee and Witch-Burner in Modern Politics

ISBN/EAN: 9783337390204

Printed in Europe, USA, Canada, Australia, Japan

Cover: Foto ©Andreas Hilbeck / pixelio.de

More available books at **www.hansebooks.com**

THE

Pharisee and Witch - Burner

IN

Modern Politics.

THE

PHARISEE AND WITCH-BURNER

IN

MODERN POLITICS.

CHAPTER I.

THE COUNTRY VOTER.

It is the design of this work to act in the mind of the reader as the rudder of a ship in the hands of a trust-worthy pilot. The ship may, in the regular and legiti-mate pursuit of its calling, touch at ports that arouse anything but pleasant emotions in the minds of some of its patrons, but for all that they have no quarrel with the rudder, whose only function is to guide the craft safely past the shoals and rocks, and mayhap the wrecks, more or less antiquated, that lie in its general course. Whatever may be the ultimate fate of the vessel, the rudder, if it shall have faithfully performed its duty at all times in the many and varied cruises of the weather-beaten hulk, can have no regrets, and must be accorded by all men what it shall have justly won, credit for doing its work conscientiously and well.

The rudder that shall pilot faithfully through the mind of the reader the craft of Truth, in connection with certain developments and innovations in our politics, will be amply satisfied if it leaves those who do it the honor to inspect the vessel, with the conviction that they have been enlightened upon things which have hitherto seemed dark and difficult of comprehension. It may be as well to state at the outset one fact as a general proposition, about the correctness of which it may be safely assumed there is no dispute, namely : That the things in politics which seem darkert and most problematical are mainly confined to large cities and towns. The saying, originating from a reverential appreciation of what appeals to our higher being in nature, that " the Creator made the country and man made the town," may suggest to the mind of the reader a general idea of the cause upon which the above stated proposition is based.

How often do we hear the assertion made by country members of a State Legislature, that "the city members want everything." That there is an assumption on the part of political leaders residing in large cities that the country members of their party are less guileless than themselves, is a fact that stands more to the credit of the country partisan than to that of his city brother.

The position of the country voter in the relation he bears to the city bred politician is somewhat peculiar. Almost a total stranger to the motives and objects which govern the political acts of the city man, he is yet a sort of "court of last resort" to which the latter appeals when he sees trouble ahead for his party. "We do not know how the country vote is going!" "We do not know what the country districts will do!" How often are these expressions heard in the closing days of an important State or National canvass, when both parties are in the height of anxiety over the question of the probable result.

As a consequence of this universal tendency on the part of city politicians, or of city residents interested in political objects, of late years to appeal to the country voters, there has been a marked increase in one of the most useful branches of our industries, the printers' business, and the country voter has received in recent political campaigns, especially in Pennsylvania, enough printed circulars, pamphlets and newspapers, gratuitously, to make it quite an object to him, provided the old junk man and all-around dealer in waste paper and rags pursues his calling in the immediate neighborhood.

It will be readily recognized by the country voter that, as he is an object of appeal for nothing less than his vote for purposes which, so far as the scope and aim of this work is concerned, have their origin in the brains of persons resident in large cities, he has a right to know something about the men who address him. Bearing in mind the fact that the city bred political man, whether he be a practical politician identified with one or other of the two parties, an amateur politician seeking notoriety to help on a precarious law business or some other calling in a condition equally unsatisfactory, or one of the ever dissatisfied dabblers in politics so hard to classify but sometimes known as Mugwumps, will equally bear close scrutiny as to the motives and objects animating them in their appeal to him, he will do well to reflect carefully before accepting what they say in their circulars, their pamphlets, or their partisan and gratuitously distributed newspapers, as unshaken and unshakable truth.

CHAPTER II.

THE FANATICAL REFORMER.

It is always difficult in a narrative which deals with matters of fact, as distinguished from matters of fiction, to convey the exact truth of any given occurrence or to represent faithfully, conscientiously and accurately, the motive which animates a person or persons in the pursuit of a given purpose. We are too ready to "jump at conclu, sions," too ready in our hurry and pre-occupation of mind to accept shallow, fleeting impressions, the indefinite outlines of the object, as conclusive evidence of its real form and nature. How often do we read in print things represented as true, which we, from our individual knowledge of the facts or circumstances, know are far from being true! How often do we hear our friends and neighbors make statements which, while we know they would not wilfully misrepresent, are known to us the moment they are uttered to be far from the truth, a knowledge which is none the less absolute by reason of our consciousness that the words are said without due reflection, and that those who thus unwittingly falsify, speak from the fleeting and deceptive surface, impressions reinforced by prejudice and preconceived opinions, which they are willing to give out as truth.

It is the consideration of such facts, perhaps, which has caused the old masters, the wise men of all ages, to echo the mournful saying, "the truth is hard." Our inherited

prejudices, our acquired habits and our temporal sur-
roundings all conspire to make us accept what is wafted
to us from afar, from the more or less uncertain sayings
of others, as the unquestioned truth, having lulled to
sleep our own powers of reflection, of comparison, of
analysis, of weighing and testing by our common-sense
and reason, without which we cannot be sure of the truth
at all.

There was a time when men believed that witches
travelled through space over a certain section of this
land balanced upon nothing less common-place than
a broom-stick, and the grim sequel to the matter
was the fact that, with the sanction and upon the
insistence of the spiritual teachers, who,—sitting in their
studies and knowing little more than infants of the great,
practical world,—sincerely believed they were right, human
beings were burned at the stake. We look back now at
the spirit of intolerance and persecution which laid poor
helpless women upon the fagots at Salem less than two
hundred years ago, and we wonder if there can be anything worse, of all the evils in the world, than an aroused
fanaticism.

It does not make the heart less full of pity for the
wretched women who met such horrible deaths in the old
Puritan town, to be told that the clergymen and the
authorities, the good people, if you please, believed themselves to be doing a heavenly duty. Their belief having
brought about a consummation of the sacrifice, they could
not restore the charred and shapeless bodies to life after

the scales had fallen from their eyes, and they found they had done atrocious murder.

Whence does this spirit of intolerance, of assuming divinely invested authority to make others do as the deluded and zealous fanat¡c himself believes, come? Not from the founder of the Christian religion, for he was all kind, all merciful, all tolerant. There is the record that he disliked the Pharisees, the men who rolled their eyes to Heaven and said, " I am holier than thou."

The spirit of intolerance comes not from the practical man, not from the workingman, not from the men who labor on farms, or in the factories or in the mill. It was not observable among the poor fishermen with whom the Christian Teacher associated, and hence he was their associate. If a man was defamed, or villified, or abused in name and reputation by the Pharisees, the Saviour of mankind did not go to them and say " well done." On the contrary he, knowing the interested motives of men, knowing men's hearts, knew well that if a person were singled out by the Pharisees for abuse and dispraise, there was more hope for such a man than there was for the zealot and high-headed ones who defamed him.

Our inherent regard for the past is apt to lead us into the error of supposing that the Pharisees of Scriptural time and the puritanic witch-burners of two hundred years ago in Massachusetts have no successors, that they were peculiar to the times in which they lived. Is this the truth? Let us see.

It only requires a survey of sixty years of the history

of Philadelphia to disclose the fact that an element of the "best citizens," including clergymen and doctors and lawyers and merchants, rose in arms when it was proposed to introduce gas through the streets. They held town meetings and issued solemn addresses against the dangerous innovation. They petitioned councils and the authorities to frown down such a hazardous scheme, as the gas would surely become ignited and the flame, running through the pipe under ground, would blow up the city and destroy the property and people.

The gas came in time and the "best citizens," the clergymen, the doctors, the lawyers and the merchants were satisfied. Nothing blew up, and their belief was changed. They found they had been too hasty, but there is no record that any of them ever openly admitted it.

Then, easily within the memory of middle-aged men now living there came another fever of puritanic intolerance and impracticability. Some of the "best citizens' were much aggrieved over the fact that the elections were not going right. They looked about and finally came to the conclusion that they had been appointed by Providence to correct the evil, and they set about with a zeal and impatience, always characteristic of such a class, to do it. The fanatic, who feels called upon to reform something, can always find his victim. This time the "best citizens," the clergymen, the doctors, the lawyers and the merchants found their victims in certain poor foreigners. Philadelphia had at that time as it has to-day, a great many Irishmen—honest, hard-working, cheerful-hearted men who had come over to the new country to better their condition, just as the ancestors of the "best citizens" had done years before.

The "best citizens" began to persecute the people of foreign birth by agitating the question of depriving them of the right to vote. They formed what was called the "Know Nothing Party." But like the opposition of their predecessors to the introduction of gas, "nothing blew up" except the "Know Nothing Party" and the "best citizens" themselves.

CHAPTER III.

SOME PHARISAIC TRAITS.

IF the Pharisee of to-day is intolerant, narrow and defamatory in matters connected with public improvements and the expenditure of money therefor, what is his disposition in the world of politics? In the temporary heat and excitement of a campaign such as the American system of politics, where every man stands upon an equality, produces, the successors of the Pharisees and witch-burners amply vindicate the spirit and doctrine of their predecessors. They acquire a notion from reading newspapers that everything is wrong in politics, and that there is a " call " for them to band themselves together, not for the purpose of going out and mingling with the people and familiarizing themselves with the facts of the matter. They have not been used to associating with the hard toilers of the world. Their ideas of politics have been gathered from reading in their cozy libraries, not American books, but English books perhaps; and it is the simple truth to say that when your Pharisee in politics sees anything in an English book or newspaper that speaks to the discredit or dispraise of politics or government, municipal, State or National, in his own country he gloats over it as if he had found a rare treasure. If the defamatory words are in a newspaper he cuts them out and carefully preserves them; if they are in a book he carefully marks the place.

And note one peculiarity about the Pharisee in politics : he would rather a hundred-fold read something derogatory to the politics of his own country in an English newspaper or book than in a newspaper or book printed in his own land. The reason is not difficult to understand. When he sees the villification in the foreign print it flatters his vanity that the mind of some one in the far away country across the water whom he has never seen nor heard of, exactly corroborates his own view of the matter. The effect of this new consciousness in him is an increased activity in the business of political witch-burning, and an increased disregard of facts and boldness of defamatory utterance. He is thenceforth a victim of Angliaphobia, and in his rabid, venomous assaults upon the character of men prominent in the politics of his country he far excels any foreign defamer of his land that the generation can produce.

Note also another reason. The Pharisee in very many cases, indeed in cases numerically in the proportion of nine to ten, wears foreign-made clothing, and is connected financially with enterprises dependent upon foreign capital. In Philadelphia, the most prominent of the political Pharisees are connected with fire and marine insurance companies which have their main offices in London or Liverpool ; or they are dealers in woolens or worsteds, and have mills and factories operated by cheap labor in England or Germany; or they are importers who have been in the habit of buying their goods from abroad for years, regardless of the fact that the growing industries of their own country can furnish as good an article and in very many cases a much better one; and they have formed a liking for everything English and foreign and acquired a prejudice against the products and the habits of the nation of their birth.

These are the "interested Pharisees." Incensed at the existing government because its policy is not such as suits their pet foreign hobbies, they seek to overturn the party in power, carefully cloaking their real motives. They attack the party of the government, defame its leaders, give hearty welcome to all publications that malign, villify and misrepresent, never once remembering the injunctions of the Christian Preceptor to " have charity for all," or to " set a seal upon thy lips."

We have spoken of this class of political zealots or witch-burners as "interested Pharisees," in order that those who are prompted in their political action, partly but not wholly, by mercenary motives, may be seen and recognized by the reader. We shall now proceed to describe the co-ordinate branch of the Pharisee tribe, who, animated by motives not mercenary, are found standing shoulder to shoulder with the others with mouths open, ever ready to emit venomous, calumnious utterances; ever ready to interpret the sayings of public men to their detriment; ever ready to throw out the crafty, cunning, cruel insinuation; ever ready to deal with harmful inuendo; ever ready to give aid and countenance to the hurtful report, and always, always more ready, more willing, more delighted to speak, hear and read of what is ill against men of prominence in public affairs than to speak, hear and read of what is in their favor.

It is not a very lovable class of mankind we have to deal with, and we fancy we can hear the reader murmur something about the justice of our rendering an apology for introducing them to him. But we feel that he has need to know them for several reasons. He should know them for one reason that he may know how much their counsel is worth. He should know them for another reason that he may know who is largely responsible for the deplorable tendency of late years to conduct our political campaigns on the basis of bitter and disgraceful personalities. He should know them also that he may be forewarned against that self-assuming, narrow element which is found in every age, and which, in self-laudatory spirit, delights in calling itself " our best citizens," just as the Pharisees of the Christian founder's time and the witch-burners of Cotton Mathers' time delighted in doing, and which feels itself called upon to reform something, not by quiet, patient work, but by perturbed, half-digested ideas and appeals, not to speak of abusive and defamatory methods.

For these reasons, among others, he should know them; and that he may know them, we shall endeavor to truthfully describe them in the next chapter.

CHAPTER IV.

ORIGIN OF MOTIVES.

It has been frequently said that when a man hoards up wealth and leaves it to his children, they will soon find means to scatter it.

This saying may be true in the main, and it may be wholly true in some localities, but not in Philadelphia. The city of Penn is essentially a city where money made by one generation is saved, and in many cases added to by another.

There are in Philadelphia some families whose ancestors made their money truck-farming and also in the ship chandlering line. The descendants of the worthy truck gardener and ship chandler are now persons of means and importance in the city. They have costly homes, ample libraries and plenty of leisure. They sit in their libraries and read much of the time, go to the opera in winter, go cruising in their yachts to the West Indies, or to Rye Beach, New Hampshire, or elsewhere in summer.

In the abundance of their leisure in their costly and beautiful homes, they get " out of joint " with the masses of the people around them. Never having occasion to soil their hands with work, they do not come in contact with the mechanic, the laboring man or the artisan. They know as little about making a living by toil as a child unborn.

These men, from the lack of something to do,

become impatient to make themselves felt in the world. They conceive the idea from reading the daily journals that something is wrong. They may have a pardonable desire to see their names in the newspapers. This is frequently the case.

They get to theorizing about government. Things are not going right politically. They have read the name of a certain leader quite frequently in the newspapers, read a great many things about him, some things not to his credit, as is very likely in cases of newspaper mention of public men. They have conceived somehow or other a dislike for him. The more they think about him the more they dislike him. They have never seen him. How could they have personal knowledge of him since they do not mingle with the masses, and know practically nothing about the affairs of the people. Their time has been taken up collecting rents, traveling in Europe, cruising in yachts and theorizing in their libraries.

Now, however, they have made up their minds to do something. The leader whom they have read about has too much power. They have begun to hate him. They readily believe everything they hear about him, no matter how bad it is. If they should be told that he had horns and hoofs they would perhaps agree that it must be so.

It is apparent that these harmless non-producers of the necessaries of life, living their easy lives on the money left them by their fathers or acquired by shrewd and worldly-wise marriages, easily have their zeal fired by the first class of Pharisees, the "interested Pharisees." The two classes band themselves together and go into politics, not as active participants in the struggle on the field, but as a "best citizens" corps, who stay by themselves and invariably take the side of the weaker party.   It is altogether a matter of sentiment with them.   They have nothing in common with the material interests of the masses of practical, struggling men, though they may in reality imagine they have, and may do good in the churches and Sabbath schools one day in a week, no matter how much defaming and " casting of first stones " and general uncharitableness they may have done in the other six days.

It is this class of men that has given us one of the most widely known, as well as one of the most popular characterizations in the English language for use in describing a particular group of persons found in almost every community, who are a little world unto themselves, and who are against everything that does not conform with their way of thinking,—"a mutual admiration society."

The sun, the moon, the stars, the great works of nature have no significance to the minds of these people.   Outside their counting rooms, where thrifty bargains are made with secret profits at the expense of country business men, that would make your ordinary political office-holder open his eyes wide in astonishment that he had something yet to learn, they have perpetual visions of receptions in fashionable dress, of the flavor of terrapin and of the opportunities which will be afforded for the display of their wealth, and the indulgence of mutual felicitation and the enjoyment of crude compliments ; for your "mutual admiration society" man is great at expressing himself in smart, glib remarks, calculated to please his fellow member.

It is perhaps no exaggeration to say that the spirit of "mutual admiration" is more fully developed among the two classes of Pharisees heretofore described in Philadelphia than among those of any other city in the Union. If the epidemic of "witch-burning" were to break out in America again it is fairly within the range of probability that it would not be in Massachusetts, nor in any part of New England, where it would first show itself, but in Philadelphia, among those Pharisees who are too good to belong to any political party, either Republican or Democratic, but who are a select band of impracticable beings endeavoring to make a 'little party of their own, by sending out pamphlets, addresses and circulars defaming public men and legislative bodies, in the hope of securing recruits.

It is not the purpose of this work to do this peculiar element of citizens any injustice, lest the tender feelings of any member of the mutually admiring group might be hurt. They are here with us with all their bowing and scraping and deferential airs and manners toward one another, and they cannot be exterminated. They have their use in the world, perhaps, even though that use has not been made apparent to men.

Yet we know how quickly they would dwindle out of sight in the presence of some great National uprising,—in the presence of a war, for example, which would call into play all the practical and great qualities of our public men, of our party leaders. It is only in long periods of peace and prosperity that the modern Pharisee in politics flourishes. He is suffering for something to do, as we have said, and he gets to theorizing. He constructs beautiful castles, the turrets of which cast their shadows into the millennium. The theories he spins in his deluded brain he believes are great truths, and he seeks to find followers to " reform the old party " or found a new one.

These Pharisees flourished in poor, care-worn Lincoln's time. They were his bitterest and most venomous assailants. The coming of the war drove them into the back-ground, whence the main portion of them emerged after Lincoln's assassination, and took their part among those who were that great man's chief mourners and eulogists.

As has been said, it is not designed to represent these persons in any light save that in which they present themselves. We try to do them justice in our description of them. We cannot find fault that they are as they are. It is natural to them. As well might we display a feeling of anger that the nature of a jackal, or of a lizard, or of a snake is what it is. We have no quarrel with the snake, or the lizard, or the jackal any more than we have a quarrel with the political Pharisee and witch-burner. He is here and he is what he is. He believes he is right, and according to his nature and his light, he is right. He defames public men, spreads the slime of his calumny and rancorous venom over them, and sleeps the sounder for it at night, feels the better for it when he goes to church; and shall we indulge in anger with him because he is simply following the bent of his nature?

We do not get angry at the snake when it hisses at us, nor at the skunk when it ejects the noisome fluid; we only avoid them. Both the snake and the skunk believe they are doing right when they thus assail us, and there is no doubt that the political Pharisee believes he is right when he traduces public men and adds to the already unhealthy atmosphere of a heated political canvass his stock of disgraceful personalities and skillfully worded insinuations.

CHAPTER V.

THE PHARISEE ON "HIGH GROUND."

LET the reader now withdraw his mind from the contemplation of that phase of the political Pharisee's nature which relates to his resemblance to the animal of the noisome vapor, and see him as he desires to be seen before the world.

He is eminently respectable in his connections and in his appearance. He frequently makes speeches on the current evils in politics, in a small squeaking voice, and no man living can take exception to the high ground upon which he builds his platform. He stands before his audience a really good man. Sometimes there are those present who are unkind enough to remark that he "broke up" this or that church and drove the minister out of the congregation because he "wanted his own way." This may be true, and it is very likely to be true of our political Pharisee, but it must be remembered he is doing what he believes to be right, although a short-sighted posterity may not realize that he ever existed.

He stands before his audience speaking from his high ground, in his small, squeaking voice, his right hand oftentimes given to the see-saw gesture. His present performance is different from writing secret defamatory pamphlets, circulars or addresses to "the voters of the State."

He talks like one who is conscious that he would have

been a shining light in the ministry, but does not, at the same time, wish to make the modest gentleman in black who sits near him, the clergyman, feel badly by excelling him in the display of his morality or his delivery, though of course, if the comparison in his favor is apparent to the eyes of the audience, he cannot help it.

The evils of politics are the crying evils of the day. The political leaders are all corrupt. They should be overthrown and good men should be put in their places and " sound political methods " should again hold sway.

As the political Pharisee delights in decrying and discrediting the politics of his country in the eyes of strangers, of foreigners, he is never satisfied with the present. He is morally certain that the generation in which he lives is the worst his city and State ever saw. He continually laments the degeneracy of the times, the decline of talent and leadership in public men. He longs for the time when his State " held a position of honor among the States of the Union."

Thus does he speak before his audience in his swallow-tail and choker, and he wins great applause and many flattering remarks.

And while he is thus talking from his " high ground," and straining his eyes to see in the future the restoration of that " honor " to his State which he claims she has lost, there is another picture that might well be placed in contrast. There sits in his home, or in a hotel away from the comforts of his home, weary and meditative, that political leader who has come in for such a great share of abuse from our truly good political Pharisee.

The hour is late, the fire in his room has burned low. Upon his table are heaps of letters and telegrams and visitors' cards, some of them torn, and their fragments littering the floor.

He has evidently had much on his mind. He sits now quiet, meditative, reflective. A knock falls upon his door. So comfortable, so restful, after his busy day, must he now be disturbed! "Come in!" he calls in a patient, even voice, which shows no sign of the irritation he first felt.

It is a humble looking caller who enters. The truly good political Pharisee would think of handing him over to a policeman if he knocked upon his door at this time of night. He is, perhaps, a middle-aged man, rather seedy in appearance, slightly embarrassed about making the object of his visit known, and rather backward generally.

"How do you do," says the political leader, whom our Pharisee has been only a few moments before so roundly abusing, yet whom he has never seen. The leader shakes the hand of his humble visitor and asks him to have a chair.

The man sits down. "What can I do for you?" asks the political leader in a kindly tone which places the caller at his ease at once.

"I'll tell you," says the visitor in an earnest voice; "I've come to see if you couldn't get me a place. I've been out of work for a long time, except a little to do here and there, and my wife is sick and I want to get something steady to do. I don't care what it is so it's work that will enable me to make a living."

" What kind of work would you like to have?" asks
the leader, taking an interest in the case at once.

The visitor tells him, and for three-quarters of an hour
the humble man who is out of employment, but who
belongs to the same party as his chief, sits there and
talks over his chances of getting work. It is only one
of twenty similar cases which have been before the
leader during the day in addition to other and more important matters.

What more important matters? Does not the political
leader have an easy time? What other matters more
important has he to look after?

Matters relating to the policies and plans of the party
organization to which he belongs which may have a con-
trolling influence in shaping the most momentous event
of the nation; matters which, when finally decided upon,
may result in bringing about the nomination and election
of a president of the greatest country on the globe; matters
which, once weighed and carefully examined by the brain
of that man who has been and is so much abused by the
political Pharisees and witch-burners, may result in turn-
ing the tide of the nation's history just as the nomination
of Lincoln over Seward, almost by an accident, brought
about one of the grandest and most glorious achievements that humanity has ever seen—freedom of four
million human beings from bondage.

The political Pharisee's bow has only one string to it,
and he thrums and thrums upon it constantly. He does
not know this political leader except through defamatory
sources of information. If the leader is a Republican,

a member of the majority party, he may have done something to incense the opposition party to the degree of
burning wrath. He may have been the means of electing
a president of his own political faith and of ousting one
who belonged to the party of the opposite faith. If that
is so, is it not probable that all the venom and spleen
and malignity which partisan hate, disappointed aspirations, thwarted ambitions, destroyed political prospects
and humbled party pride can produce, have been con-
centrated upon that one shining leader of the hated
opposition party to break him down, destroy his power
and cripple the great political army which he lately led
to victory.

Have people ears, and do they not hear?   Have they
eyes, and do they not see?

But to return to the two pictures!—of our political
Pharisee, with his swallow-tail and choker, the truly good
man that he is, talking to his select audience from his
"high ground" about the evils of politics ; and our political leader in his room after a busy day, during which his
brain was employed upon matters that may change the
course of history in a country of nearly seventy million
people. The leader has had time, great as has been
the nature of the business on which his mind was
engaged, to take up one of the most simple and ordinary
affairs of life—the helping of a poor man to find a situation whereby he can make a living for himself and
family—and he is giving that matter just as much attention, just as earnest an effort in proportion, as if it were
an affair of the nation. He succeeds presently in getting

the man a position in the service of the City, State or
National Governments, and the moment the appointment is
made public the Pharisee denounces it as another
evidence of the political leader's unfitness to occupy the
position he holds, and forthwith either calls a meeting of
his committee to condemn it, issues a circular protesting
against it, or gets up a type-written interview with himself inveighing against it,—which interview usually starts
out with the statement that he was very much disin-
clined to talk,—and sends it to all the newspapers for
publication.

CHAPTER VI.

A QUESTION OF RIVALRY AS CURATIVES.

WE should like to digress here for a moment from the main theme, and invite the reader to deliberate with us upon what seems a serious problem, as between the political Pharisee with the squeaking voice and the swallow-tail and choker, and the political leader and his practical methods, as to the efficacy of the two men respectively, applying them as remedies for the two most common ills that afflict a great many members of the human family—hunger and lack of work.

Let us suppose that the timid, discouraged seeker after work to keep himself and family from starving, instead of going to the political leader,—with his practical, good-hearted ways, living in the present and dealing with the present in practical fashion,—had betaken himself to the political Pharisee, with his mind in the past or future and with his voice singing the mournful strain that things were not as they used to be, that the standard of honor among public officials was not as high and that his State was a by-word and reproach among men.

The poor man in search of labor, with the wife and hungry children dependent upon him, would perhaps feel that he could stand the imaginary degeneracy of the honor of his times and his State with somewhat more satisfaction than he could bear the prospect of finding no bread.

The political Pharisee would hardly give the seeker after labor the opportunity to see him. He already has calls upon his charity. He is constantly giving money to alleviate the condition of the Indians. He cannot be expected to do more. He has even given valuable time and money to have an investigation made in order to determine whether this government which he finds so much fault with in the hands of the present political party, has been doing justice to the Indians. If there were no Indians in the country his charity perhaps would be applied to some of Stanley's dwarf races in Darkest Africa. For the political Pharisee is a great man for doing good after his own fashion.

In this work we have endeavored to give every side of the character appertaining to the Pharisee that has any bearing upon or relation to the public. There is one phase of the subject however, upon which we have not touched, and yet it is one of the most conspicuous and important of all his traits and characteristics.

The political Pharisee invariably claims to be a Republican anxious to reform his party. He does not associate with the Democrats. There are no Democratic political Pharisees. Nobody living ever saw one. The Pharisee professes to believe, righteous man that he is, that the Democratic party is too bad for anybody to belong to. The burden of his life is the fear that if the Republican party is not purged of its corrupt leaders, his City and State will go Democratic. The prospect of this dreadful calamity brings tears to his eyes no doubt. They have not been seen by any known witnesses, but there is no question that it is so, for he is always deploring a possible Democratic result, and it is clear that " where there is so much smoke, there must be some fire."

This habit of the political Pharisee and witch-burner of classing himself as a Republican, is one of his striking peculiarities.   It is a sure indication of his character.

CHAPTER VII.

PHARISAIC STOLEN LIVERY.

IF there be any virtue in the practice of organizing political parties and of abiding with them after they have been organized, what position does the political Pharisee assume when he rails against party men and party leaders and sees merit only in the decision of the party man to yield to his importunate requests to desert his party and ally himself with his views and objects?

Desert his party for what? Not that he may change his political belief. The Pharisee does not ask him; he scorns the idea that he should be considered capable of asking him, to become a Democrat. He asks him only to vote for the candidates of the Democratic party. His central thought and hope are that the candidate of his own party, or of the party to which he claims to belong, shall be defeated.

In due course of time the election takes place and the Pharisee's wish is gratified. The Republican party has been defeated. Democracy has been triumphant.

Another election period approaches. Again the political Pharisee, who may be supposed to be still farther than ever alienated from his former party associates, espouses the cause of the Democratic candidate. This time his hope is not realized. The Democratic candidate is defeated and Republicanism is triumphant.

The Pharisee, further than ever outside the pale of his

former organization, again makes common cause with the Democracy. He sends out solemn circulars and appeals not to Democrats, but to Republican voters and signs himself "a Republican voter."

There are some deceptions which are practiced year after year upon an ordinarily wide-awake public by designing persons and no word of protest is uttered. What greater imposition on the confidence of honest men can be carried into effect than the one just described? How long shall a man, who imagines himself too good to stay within the folds of his party, and who engages openly in advocating and otherwise seeking the election of a candidate of the opposite organization, be justified in holding the name of the party to which he once belonged? Why does he cling to that party name when his acts, and thoughts, and opinions have been and are henceforth altogether hostile to it? Why does he send out circulars and appeals to honest and unsuspecting voters of the party in which he originally held membership, invoking their aid and co-operation in his destructive work against that party, and sign himself "a Republican?"

Is he a Republican? Does the common sense of men assert itself in his case and recognize the falsehood, the willful design to mislead which is wholly invested in his claim? He has been voting for Democratic candidates for ten years past, with perhaps one or two exceptions. There have been two tickets a year placed before him for the exercise of his suffrages, making twenty in the entire period, and he has voted for three Republican tickets and for seventeen Democratic tickets. In the name of common sense and reason why does he sign himself in his circulars and petitions addressed to the voters of the party to which he once bore allegiance, " a Republican ? "

Why does he not openly and in manly fashion go over to the Democratic party in name as he does in act ? Is he ashamed of that party and therefore desirous of doing his part to aid it secretly because of that shame ? If not, what reason can he give for assuming the covert, skulk- ing attitude that belongs not to honorable, courageous, practical men, but to creeping, cowering traitors ?

CHAPTER VIII.

THE PHARISEE'S " BLACK BEAST."

THE literary style of the political Pharisee has become so familiar in his prodigal use of pamphlets, circulars and addresses of late that any one reasonably conversant with recent political campaigns, especially in Pennsylvania, can almost repeat some of them by heart.

This work would perhaps be deemed incomplete if we refrained from furnishing an example of the literary work of the gentleman who, voting constantly for the Democratic, Independent or Prohibition tickets, always signs himself " a Republican." In pursuance of the desire to enlighten the reader as to the character of the matter he usually sends out we extract some passages from a recent pamphlet which has been the product of his brain, the object of which is an assault on a political leader who has been a shining mark for the Pharisee for some months past and the nature of whose offending has been in reality the management of the last Republican National campaign in such able and skillful manner as to bring about the election of a Republican President.

The pamphlet, according to its title, is "An Address to the Citizens of Pennsylvania Protesting Against Quayism in the Republican Party." It reads—and we call upon the reader to note carefully the truly good professions which it makes as to its motives—as follows:

"As Pennsylvanians, and as Republicans, we, the undersigned, feel constrained to address our fellow-citizens throughout the State upon the present political situation, —to point out what we believe to be the essential causes of the alarming degradation in public affairs from which we now suffer, and the necessary steps toward improvement.

"The Republican machine in this State, under the leadership of Senator Quay and those lieutenants whom he has drawn about him, is corrupt and in strong contrast with the rank and file of the party. That leadership is as absolute in its control as it is unscrupulous in its methods and disastrous in its results. With Senator Quay's political record the public is so familiar that it is unnecessary at this time to give a detailed history of those more remote public acts through which its notoriety was acquired, while a brief reference to its more recent events is appropriate in order to detect clearly the present situation."

The " address " then goes on to arraign this Republican leader for many and various acts. It charges him with being responsible for the " overwhelming disaster which befell the Republican party in this State during the past autumn "—which is, perhaps, one of the most amazing examples of effrontery yet furnished by queer humanity, since the Pharisees themselves were in the main responsible for that " overwhelming disaster " in having worked and voted for the Democratic candidate for governor.

The address continues, and finally, pausing to take breath from its hot pursuit after Senator Quay, as a diversion assails the last Republican legislature. It talks in favor of "reform within the party," and yet the writer of it and all his fellow Pharisees afterward united and opposed the election of the Republican candidate for Treasurer of Philadelphia, in the campaign of November, 1891, although he had been one of the most earnest, consistent and faithful reform workers Philadelphia had ever seen, and one of the original members of the Committee of One Hundred. The Pharisees found reason for opposing him in the fact that he had been nominated by the Republican Convention—a great concession to reform and a great opportunity to enforce the doctrine of "reform within the party." The Pharisaic malcontents, however, preferred the Democratic candidate, and worked, sent out tickets, and voted for him.

In the light of the true character of these persons, their "address to the citizens of Pennsylvania" against Senator Quay, seems amazing. It does not require a philosopher to see the ridiculous contrast between themselves and the party leader who is the object of their venom. There is something inexpressibly ludicrous in their position, when we reflect that one hundred years from now, if one of their old "addresses" should come to light, posterity will be well acquainted with the name of Quay, but it will have to wrinkle its brows for awhile before it can recall the name of any of his traducers. Men do not acquire the commanding position and the power held and wielded by Senator Quay by chance, any more than great generals attain their prominence and fame by chance. There must be merit, there must be power of mind, qualities of discernment, accurate judgment of men and things, a cool head and a practical application of means to ends. If our Pharisees should, by the common consent of the people and of the leaders of the people, be elevated to the commanding position of Senator Quay and of other public men, we should likely see for a time a queer country and a queer sort of government.

We could calculate upon one of them at least devoting the energies and resources of the government primarily to the care and benefit of the Indians of the far West, regardless of the fact that the poor and hungry whom we have amongst us in the East might be prostrate and crying on his door-step, for bread. There is so much more opportunity for notoriety in making the bestowal of charity upon the distant Indians our pet hobby than in quietly looking after and providing for the needs of the poor in our own immediate vicinity.

The signatures to this "address to the people of Pennsylvania" against Senator Quay will bear studying. There is a "provisional committee of nine members. Of this number three of them are known to have voted against James G. Blaine for President, one more ran for office in the Autumn of 1881, upon an Independent ticket with Democratic endorsement, and perhaps not one of them has voted the Republican ticket successively in the past five years.

The "provisional committee," which, by the way, assumes somewhat the manner of a committee of safety in the days of the French revolution, announces that it has three hundred and twenty-two names to its address against Mr. Quay. The names and addresses of the signers are given and an analysis of them reveals the fact that only eighty-one of them reside outside Philadelphia. The grappling hooks of the Pharisees do not seem to have caught an overload of " innocents " out in the State. Perhaps the native honesty of the country voter gave him a clear insight into the true motives of these men who claim to be Republicans while voting the Democratic, Independent and Prohibition tickets steadily for years past, and seeking to demoralize and belittle party organization so far as it is Republican, in order to satisfy wounded vanity and disappointed ambition.

Once more let the reader reflect that one hundred years from now this manifestation on the part of our political Pharisees and witch-burners, if a photograph of the times could be preserved for posterity, will appear even more laughable than it is now. One hundred years from now nobody conversant with his country's history will need to ask who Senator Quay was, while there will be none who can give the name of any one of the political Pharisees who are his traducers, fluttering now so aimlessly in their newly pressed swallow-tails and chokers, like a crate full of excited black-birds disturbed over the dire prospect of an eagle sweeping down upon them, and inflicting what to their distorted little brains seems like indescribable horrors.

CHAPTER IX.

A QUESTION OF PEOPLE'S RIGHTS.

THAT the influence of the political Pharisee is detrimental to the politics of a community, that one of the direct effects of his acts is to fetter the hands of a political organization in its reaching out for proper men for office and for better methods in politics, must be obvious to all who observe his conduct and note the obstinate trait in his character which refuses to be satisfied with anything that comes from the Republican leaders, whether it be a candidate or a measure of legislation, regardless of the essential question of their merits.

It must be remembered that in dealing with him we are not discussing a being possessed of the faculty of reasoning impartially, but are treating of a one-sided and oftentimes bloodless species of man who may be most fitly described, not as a person, but as an organism. He is here among us,—a factor, at present, in our politics,—an element of discord outside the lines of party organization. Elevate him to office, elect him to the Legislature or to Congress, or place him in any position where he shall be able, if he chooses, to command and distribute official patronage.

In such position, what may we reasonably assert shall be the experience of the party man or of the party worker who may seek him out and request his aid toward obtaining a place in government employ to the end that he may gain a livelihood for himself and his family.

It requires no extensive effort of the imagination to see the Pharisee draw himself up with superb dignity, or contract himself with sudden frigidity of manner, and inform the seeker after position, with scant ceremony, that he has not been elected to public position to find offices for people.

No. He has not been elected to office for that purpose; but holding official position, as he does, he is a public man and must expect applications to him from people, irrespective of "creed, color or condition," for aid in various directions.

His answer to the seeker after place, however, describes a trait in his character in the possession of which he prides himself as much, perhaps, as in any that are among his characteristics. He is not in the habit of boasting, but he will tell his friends with much modest relish, in the recollection of the high ground he occupies, how his privacy was invaded and his sense of propriety offended by a visit from a "fellow" who desired the Pharisaic official to find him a situation because he had worked and voted for him. His friends, in their social gatherings, where such experiences are usually retailed, sympathize with him and express regret that his sacred person should have been threatened with contamination through possible contact with a being such as the "political fellow" who sought an appointment.

The satisfaction of the Pharisee and his friends might be something we could sympathize with if it were the whole story and did not have the uncomfortable possibility of possessing another side. There is the not remote likelihood, however, that the man who applied for position may be miserably poor and wretched, with a wife and children dependent upon him and with no bread in the house for their hungry mouths ; with no fire or fuel in the house to warm their shivering bodies ; with no warm clothing on their backs ; with no shoes for their feet and without the means to pay for the barest and meanest of the necessaries of life.

And the wife and children must go cold and hungry, the husband and father must go about a wanderer, weary, disheartened and haggard, because of the high ground assumed by the Pharisaic office-holder !

It is one of the invariable rules of the theorist and moralist to condemn the workers in a political party, the army of active men in an organization, for their part in aiding and advancing the success of leaders whom the theorist himself considers the embodiment of all that is bad in party politics, according to the information he has received, mainly through partisan and prejudiced channels.

It might not be out of place to ask him, in view of his belief in the direction mentioned, if he has ever taken time to deliberate over the position occupied by the plain, common people of this Republic, with reference to their relations toward the leaders of their political organizations and the officers of the town, city, county, State and National governments. His consideration of the matter will doubtless remind him that the government under which he lives rests, not on tradition or precedent, but on the suffrages, on the will of the citizens, who are paramount in the exercise of the primary power. The men they elect to public position are their servants, chosen by the decision of the majority to do the work necessary for the operation of the government under the Constitution and the laws.

The relation between master and servant being what it is, shall any one say it is not the right and the privilege of the citizen, whether he be a worker in a party or not, to go to the political leader or to the office-holder and seek a place in the service of the local, State, or National governments? To deny that he possessed such right would be to deny that his country is free, in fact, as it is in name. To accept the doctrine of the Pharisee and the theorist is to curtail the citizen of the privilege he enjoys of free and unobstructed access to his official representatives, and to create an aristocracy in office-holding that would be at variance with one of the cardinal principles of the American political system,—rotation in office.

If the Pharisee complains that men of his kind are not elected to office, that they are not chosen to high and honorable political positions, his complaint, all the facts being considered, carries with it the condemnation of himself and his class. The plain citizens of the land, jealous of the preservation of their rights, will not trust him nor them. The narrowness of his mind, his contracted beliefs, his want of judgment of men, his over-estimate of his own importance, the petty motives which govern his political acts,—all combine to make him, in the eyes of the people, an undesirable person to have in charge of public affairs.

The folly of the claim which he makes, that public officers should not be applied to by persons seeking positions, that they should be placed far above the reach of influences which might serve to govern them in the matter of making appointments, seems to demand some special notice. A survey of the entire question, involving in the process a contrast between the American party man and the people of foreign countries in the relation they bear toward their governmental leaders, will show how happy is the condition of the people of this Republic in the possession of the very rights which the Pharisee condemns. No barrier is thrown across the way of the American citizen, however humble, when he seeks admittance to the presence of the American official, however great.

How happy, how thrice blessed, would the Russian peasant consider himself did he enjoy the same privileges in his own land! How rich, how complete would be the sum of his delight if he could gain access to the officers of the government under which he lives as easily as the humblest American can approach the governmental heads of this Republic.

The "high ground" about which the political Pharisee has so much to say, means the placing of the business of government and of office-getting far beyond the reach of the masses of the citizens; means the meeting of a select few persons in secret conference, in parlor or private club room, for the purpose of choosing the men they would have in office, regardless of the wishes of the people. If an injustice is done the Pharisee in this assertion, we áre not aware of it, and feel assured that no one conversant with recent political history in Philadelphia is aware of it. There does not seem to be any way in which he can explain or excuse the secret conferences and open promulgations which have been the result of them, and which are now part of Philadelphia's political history. If such conferences and promulgations do not place the Pharisee in the position of being desirous of curtailing the constitutional political rights of the people, there can be no meaning in words and no evidence in the existence of undisputed facts.

CHAPTER X.

SOME PHARISAIC INCONSISTENCIES.

IT has been shown that the Pharisaic personage in politics has one invariable claim which he parades conspicuously, which is the regulation badge of his profession,—he is "a Republican," never a Democrat.

Yet the common sense of men will readily perceive through the halo of his righteous profession the unquestioned fact of his destination politically; will easily discern the political faith of the party and of the candidates whose cause he espouses and who are the undoubted beneficiaries of his devoted and self-sacrificing work. If there is an instance on record, since the appearance of this anomaly in modern politics, of the operation of his hostility against any organization save the one which he professes to be a member of, and which he avows so much devotion for, it is not within the universal knowledge of men any more than it is within the consciousness of the party which receives the benefit of his disaffection and which, by a skillful play upon his vanity and self-importance, uses him for the promotion and advancement of its own ends while it secretly makes sport of his weakness and despises the assumption of his motives.

Professing to abhor that party, to loathe its doctrines and the character of the masses of its followers, he is ever on hand at the beginning of a political canvass to issue his addresses and pamphlets in favor of its candidates, and against the nominees of the organization he pretends to love so much even though they may have been taken from the ranks of the most trusted and most useful of reform committees; nay, may have been taken from the very reform body of which the Pharisee himself is a member, as was the case when the Republican party of Philadelphia nominated for City Treasurer, George D. McCreary, of the old Committee of One Hundred,—a man noted for innumerable public-spirited and charitable acts, and one who had sacrificed time, money and personal comfort in order that the politics of his city might be purified and proper men selected for public office.

There was at once the breaking away of old reform friends, the hurrying of old reform co-workers and fresh recruits, whose names were unknown to reform labor as well as to local fame, to secret conference, there to debate and formulate and promulgate, not in the interest of this sincere and earnest reformer, whose unselfish work of years was known to them so well, but for the benefit of the Democratic candidate.*   The man with whom they

---

* A review of some of the more conspicuous of the mistakes which have been made by Herbert Welsh's Independent committee, working in the interest of the Democratic candidate for City Treasurer, may not be untimely.   They are as follows:—

"Herbert Welsh sent a letter to his brother member of the Citizens' Committee of Fifty, William H. Rhawn, asking him for a contribution to help elect Mr. Wright, and Mr. Rhawn wrote a sharp letter back, stating that he was opposed to Mr. Wright and would do all he could for Mr. McCreary. A spirited controversy arose between the two Independents, in the course of which Mr. Rhawn told Mr. Welsh that the latter belonged to the Democratic party anyhow and not to the Republican party.

had stood shoulder to shoulder in waging timely and well-fought battles against official venality and corruption, whose purse was ever open to them when the need of means to prosecute fraud and expose crime threatened to impede their praise-worthy efforts, had lived to see the leaders of his party bow in submission to the justice of

---

"Herbert Welsh sent a letter to George Watson, of the old Committee of One Hundred, asking for a contribution for Mr. Wright, and Mr. Watson wrote back refusing him, and saying he was for McCreary, and that the position of Mr. Welsh and other 'Independents' in antagonizing such a good man amazed him.

"Herbert Welsh sent a letter to William Potter, of the old Committee of One Hundred, asking for a contribution for Mr. Wright, and Mr. Potter wrote back refusing, and saying he would do all he could to help elect George D. McCreary, 'the kind of man the reformers had sought to have nominated for public office for years.'

"Herbert Welsh sent a letter to John C. Watt, of the old Committee of One Hundred, asking for a contribution for Mr. Wright, and Mr. Watt refused and said his money and efforts should go to help elect George D. McCreary.

"Herbert Welsh sent a letter to L. G. Fouse, one of the staunchest and most uncompromising independents and reformers in Philadelphia, asking for a contribution for Mr. Wright, and Mr. Fouse wrote back, scoring Mr. Welsh and his committee for opposing Mr. McCreary, 'the kind of nominee the reformers have desired ever since the reform movement began.'

"Herbert Welsh sent a letter to W. Durell Shuster, a well-known independent business man, asking for a contribution for Mr. Wright, and Mr. Shuster wrote back a scathing letter, saying his money and efforts should go to help George D. McCreary.

"Herbert Welsh sent a letter to William C. Hannis, one of the best known Independents in the city, asking for a contribution for Mr. Wright, and Mr. Hannis came out and announced that he did not favor Mr. Wright, but that he considered the cause of reform would be best served by the election of George D. McCreary."—*Phila. Press, Oct. 25, 1891.*

his and their pains-taking and laborious work; had lived
to see them come before him in subdued spirit and absolute self-denial and say in effect: "Our party is your
party. It has been purged by you and yours and we are
content, for your interest was the interest of the people
and without the people the party must fail. We have come
to you in peace and concord to ask you, as the representatives of the great party which you have purified, to
consent to accept the position of Treasurer of the City,
knowing the people's welfare, and hence the party's welfare, will be promoted by your acceptance of this trust.
We respectfully await your answer and in the name of
our common party we ask you to not say no."

There was the triumph of men over methods, the
triumph of principle over pretense. If the object of this
remarkable solicitation loved the principles of his party,
what course was left open to him in the presence of the
proposition sent him by the unanimous voice of that
party? If he had ever harbored in his mind a just and
reasonable determination to battle against the methods of
his party so long as it should oppose a reform, what re-
mained for him to do after it had yielded completely, and
as a token of the sincerity of its new and better awaken-
ing had besought him to aid it in its higher counsel by
consenting to occupy in its name one of the most important and responsible of the trusts reposing within the
gift of the people?

Did he, being a sincere reformer and a lover of the
principles of the party, whose methods alone he had
formerly objected to, dare refuse the offer under the cir-

cumstances? That it was not convenient for him to accept any public office, that the idea of holding public position was not in harmony with his tastes and his habits, were considerations entitled to weight and influence if their operation was confined to persons indifferent on the question of politics or of the principles of a party. Applied to the case of a conscientious man, a public-spirited man, a true lover of the principles and of the past achievements of the political party to which he belonged, zealous for its welfare, possessed of motives entirely disinterested, what should the common sense and the reason of the average citizen expect his answer would be when his party, in submissive and yielding spirit, acknowledged that he was right and asked him to help guide it according to his wholesome beliefs and sound judgment?

He would have forfeited the right to the confidence and respect of his fellow Republicans had he refused, and have raised in their minds forever a doubt as to the sincerity of the motives actuating him in his past reform work. He would have proved by his act, before the eyes of all unprejudiced men, that he was not a lover of the organization in which he professed to hold membership; that he was, at heart, a sympathizer and well-wisher of the opposition party, though wearing the garb of a Republican.

He did the thing which involved the greatest self-sacrifice when he consented to stand as the candidate of his party for the office of City Treasurer. He turned his back upon the easier and more comfortable course and accepted the least pleasant and most difficult. It might be supposed, to the credit of human nature and to the encouragement of true reform in the future, that this shining member of their own band having been singled out for responsible and important public position where his influence and his work would be still more useful in elevating the political standards of his party, the old associates of the nominee would rally around him with words of praise and gladness and lighten the burden of the sacrifice he had already made by carrying him joyously and enthusiastically to the official chair, the tender of which was such a complete and absolute vindication of the justness of their worthy and long-applied efforts.

Instead of a spectacle such as we might have been prone to imagine, the reality presented a somewhat different picture. The existing organization, "The Citizens Committee of Fifty for a New Philadelphia," was divided on the question of its support between Mr. McCreary, the Reform Republican, and Mr. Wright, the Democratic nominee. Not satisfied, however, with a divided organization, the Pharisaic portion of it, led by a zealot, whose inherited wealth made him a personage of importance among men who attach weight to the possession of riches, went outside the organization and formed a new committee " for the election of the Democratic candidate for City Treasurer."

It may be as well to observe that the promoter of this new order, while professing loudly—in type-written interviews, which found their way in some singular manner to the newspaper offices, and in solemn addresses issued to the public,—to be "a Republican" desirous of "reform within the party," was unknown in the sphere of municipal reform in the discouraging days prior to the clearance of the political atmosphere by George McCreary and his associates. Coming upon the scene as a latter-day reformer and inspired by an overwhelming love of notoriety, he at once jostled aside old and tried workers and leaders, and as the head of various committees and sub-committees into which he quickly forced himself, began to launch addresses, appeals, pronunciamentos and solemn promulgations upon the public, always as "a Republican."

On one hand he had his new organization for the defeat of McCreary and the promotion of Democratic success; on the other, a second organization for the dethronement of Senator Quay, more than a year hence, by the defeat of future candidates for the legislature, to the end that such future candidates may not have the opportunity to sit in the assembly chamber and vote for the Senator's return to the United States Senate; and still further, he had his reforming interests in the Committee of Fifty to maintain.

It is to the credit of true reform that the "Committee of Fifty" should have had members in its ranks who refused to espouse the cause of the Democratic candidate and of his party.* It is to the credit of human nature

---

* "Your esteemed favor of the 15th inst. duly received. In my letter of the 7th inst., replying to yours of the 20th ult., I sought no controversy, but merely desired to explain to you why I could not unite with you and other

and to the common-sense of men as well as a solace to
the sense of wrong and injustice, which right-minded
persons feel in the presence of things done for the pre-
tended good of their fellow beings, under the mask that
veils hypocrisy, bigotry, uncharitableness, evil report,
envy, jealousy and malice, that these men uttered ringing
words of protest against the revelation of fanaticism and
two-fold motives governing the Pharisees with whom

gentlemen in the endorsement of the Democratic candidate for City Treasurer, to which you invited me.   You fail to show that your honest Democrat
would be any less under the influence of the leaders of his party than the
honest Republican would be under the leaders of his.   No one having a
knowledge of human nature could for a moment believe that either would be
absolutely uninfluenced by all party considerations whatever.   An entirely
non-partisan candidate is, at this time, an impossibility.   Therefore, the
difference between us is simply that you are more willing to trust your
honest man with the leaders of the Democratic party, where, perhaps, you
now really belong, while I prefer to trust my honest man with the leaders
of the Republican party.   If it is merely a choice between the Republican
machine and the Democratic machine, you will have to convince me, as
you seem to have convinced yourself and others with you, that the latter is
the better of the two, as I do not believe it.

  "Your reference to the Committee of Fifty I think an unfortunate one
for you.

  "While the question of the endorsement of the two candidates for the
office of City Treasurer was already in the hands of the committee for consideration, you and other members circulated your letter of endorsement
among its members and others as a confidential communication, thereby
covertly seeking to forestall the action of the committee by manufacturing a
sentiment within and without the committee in favor of the Democratic
candidate through said communication, which you having expressly re-
quested should be held as confidential, could not be openly discussed and
answered or even disclosed by gentlemen until you saw fit to make it public.

  "This appears to me to place you in the position of taking an unfair ad-

they found themselves leagued. Their eyes were soon opened to the fact that their Pharisaic brothers, who signed themselves individually " a Republican," were in reality persons who had rejected Republican candidates for no less office than the Presidency, aiding the Democratic cause in some instances by voting the Democratic ticket direct, and·in other cases by voting for the candidate of the Prohibitionists.*

---

vantage of the Republican candidate and of those members of the committee who favored his candidacy. After the matter had been brought up in the Committee of Fifty and had been referred to its Executive Committee for consideration and report, such action upon the part of the members of the committee appears to me indefensible, as thereafter any harmonious action in the committee in behalf of either candidate became impossible."— *Wm. H. Rhawn, of Citizens' Committee of Fifty, to Herbert Welsh.—Phila. Bulletin, October 19th, 1891.*

*" I congratulate the Republican party upon your nomination for the office of City Treasurer, and sincerely hope that the choice may be ratified by the people. The attitude of the Independent Republicans amazes me. If they should succeed, then what hope is there for reform in the party, whichever party it be? It seems to me simply the part of patriotism, when the dominant party nominates a gentleman who has the unbounded confidence of the people, to put the seal of public approbation upon its choice. What have Independent Republicans been insisting upon for years? Has it not been the selection of nominees by the people and not by the "bosses?" And now, when their cry has been heeded, they turn against their party to rend it.

" I have yet to learn that Mr. Wright has ever been noted for zeal in the work of political reform. I have for several years been a free lance in politics, that is so far as my vote is concerned, but I now feel that personal consistency is at stake.

" I hope you will be elected by such a majority as will prove that devotion to the good of the people is the keynote of municipal patriotism."—*Letter from Rev. Dr. William Swindells to George D. McCreary, Philadelphia Star, Oct. 19, 1891.*

They discovered likewise that the uncompromising disaffection of the majority of the Pharisees was due to their disbelief in the efficacy of the Republican doctrine that maintains a tariff on imported foreign products. Some of the Pharisaic advocates of the Democratic nominee were engaged in the mercantile line and felt that they had to pay too much duty on hosiery and woolens; others were in the business of importing groceries, and still others were officers of foreign marine insurance companies whose trade was enhanced in proportion with the increase in the shipment to this country of foreign cargoes, and all were persons whose individual pecuniary interests would be best served by the success of the Democratic party with its policy of free trade.

We have not spoken of the interested professional element attached to the Pharisaic train,—of the young lawyer with his eye shrewdly on the main chance, ever ready to catch a new client among the worthy business men; ever on the alert to "get business" out of the more mature of the mutually admiring group. The thrifty lawyer and insurance man—and perhaps the real estate man—are equally desirous of serving on committees, and they will not mind taking a chairmanship or two, particularly if it gives them notoriety, places their names in the newspapers, and above all brings them into close relations with those wealthy business men of the Pharisaic order who, mayhap, will employ them outside the hours of the reform conference, to look after odds and ends of business and do work not especially relished by the old family legal adviser or conveyancer.

The interested professional ones in the group may be mentioned as possessing one striking characteristic. They are all particularly defamatory and vindictive in their speech against prominent Republican leaders. They find it is a popular thing to talk against Quay, and they mention the name of that much abused Senator so often with venom and dispraise that an observant physiognomist might discern a slight change in the form of their mouths due to the constant use of gutterals in the expression of their disgust and hatred of the man whom it is so popular to hate and abuse.

Nor is it strange that it should be popular among this class, for without that Republican leader there would have been no Republican President, and no tariff to plague and fret "a Republican," with his business profits depending on the maintenance of his foreign marine insurance business; on his ability to import his hosiery and woolens and groceries free of duty. Let the Pharisaic camp therefore resound with defamation against Quay and Quayism; let the young lawyer and the real estate man and the keen-eyed insurance man vie with each other in spreading evil report against this hated man, for it is very popular among their patrons, as sweet music to their ears, and the great masses of the people who know not their motives any more than they know their characters—save through the medium of their truly good addresses beginning with "we, the undersigned Republicans"—will be duly impressed by their zeal and the quality of their denunciation of the late chairman of the Republican National Committee, whose political generalship made such bad, not to say keenly disappointed prophets of them in the presidential campaign of 1888.

CHAPTER XI.

THE PHARISEE VERSUS LABOR.

THE honorable and intellectual business of pleading the law has been from time unreckoned an avocation subject to the criticism of men, to slight remark, to the indulgence of the propensity of mankind to jest and make display of small wit, regardless of the question of the extent of experience or of knowledge the critics may possess of the profession they defame and against which they so readily affect a willingness to bear evil report. This prejudice against a calling as old almost as social government itself, is illustrated in the present day by the existence of a clause in the constitution of the greatest workingmen's organization perhaps that America has ever known, the Knights of Labor, which proscribes lawyers from fellowship in the order, a curious instance of the practical application of the bias in the judgment of men, that obtains among those who labor with their hands against a class of citizens, more or less learned, who are part of the remaining numbers of the human family who rely for subsistence upon the work of their heads.

It is possible, if these same Knights of Labor could hear, in moments of freedom of mind and disinterested attention, the bitter complaints of many of the younger and of the less successful members of the learned profession which they appear to discountenance, to the effect that " the trust companies with their title insurance and

conveyancing departments have ruined the law business "
they would experience a change in the view, or at least
a modification of the feeling they now entertain toward
lawyers as a class.

The evidence of the ability of many of the learned
members of the labor-order-proscribed calling to adapt
means to ends, however, is shown with striking conclu-
siveness by the eagerness with which they betake themselves to the " conference of our best citizens to devise
ways and means to reform our party." It might be
uncharitable to suggest that among those who respond
to the call for such affairs there is usually to be found an
element in the legal talent represented which has been
unsuccessful in finding satisfaction for its personal ambitions and political aspirations in any party, and therefore
readily assents to the proposition that the party which
is most powerful and which could most easily have
bestowed its favors upon it is in need of reforming.

The motive which actuates men, however, is not always
clear to the disinterested spectator, and when solemn and
almost lugubrious addresses are issued " to the citizens "
assailing or arraigning a party or a party's leaders or both,
with an appeal to those citizens to note the array of
respectable names which support the address, the respect-
ability may be more observable than the motive which
·prompts the signature. The citizen is wise, therefore,
who refrains from accepting the invitation or the advice
embodied in the address until he shall have deliberated
and taken time to inquire into the possible motives of those
who do him the honor to seek his co-operation in their

grandly pictured work. He may not allow himself to be influenced solely by the claim that the names of the signers are eminently respectable, for respectable men have been known once or twice in the world's history to be insincere, one-sided, narrow, prejudiced, selfish, impracticable, uncharitable and to be guilty likewise—always for the good of the object they seek—of prevarication. There is no evidence that the man Dives, of Scriptural mention, was anything other than respectable, and it is possible that while he slighted the beggar at his door he may have been noted for his donations to, and his grave concern for, the welfare of the Indians or equivalent tribes in the remote dominions of his country.

If we may recur to that pamphlet heretofore alluded to, "an address to the citizens of Pennsylvania," promulgated against the Republican party and United States Senator Quay by certain gentlemen in Philadelphia, and in a few counties outside, who preface their address with "We, the undersigned Republicans," it will not be untimely to say that of the 322 signatures which the promoters of the address succeeded in obtaining, up to September, 1891, after nearly a year's work, thirty-three of them are lawyers,—a proportion of more than ten per cent. of members of a single profession on a list, where the followers of all vocations and pursuits, save that of laboring with the hands, are supposed to be represented.

That the labor people are unrepresented on the address is not surprising since the fact of the preponderance of representation of the legal profession is sufficient, if there were no other reason, to cause them to look upon the motives which inspire the movement with proper suspicion. If the lawyer is excluded from the noted labor organization and readily admitted to the Pharisaic political committee, it may be in order to observe that the fundamental beliefs and aims of the two bodies are radically different, not to say wholly antagonistic.

The latter body seeks to build up a political element that will reform the party it claims to love, but which it will, for the present, sacrifice, by using the material which has been rejected by the former, as an important part of the composition which enters into its structure.

With its array of three hundred and twenty-two names, thirty-three of them being lawyers, it appeals to the citizens of a State in which exist more assemblies of the gigantic labor order, that will have nothing to do with lawyers, than is to be found in any other State in the Union, and asks them to join with it in a new political reformation.

The intelligence of unprejudiced men, whether, they labor with their hands or with their heads, will see the ridiculous aspect of the movement and note the insincerity and inconsistency of its professions as well as the impracticability of its aims.

The men engaged in it may be truly good, in the sense of the child who knows no wrong, and may believe with ready credence all the defamation and slander borne upon the poisonous political winds to the alert sense of their waiting and horrified ears. They may likewise possess a simply human love of publicity, in the indulgence of which they will not stop, good and righteous as they are, to promote the circulation of the slander or to swell the tide of villification against men whom they have never seen but against whom their enmity, fed by hear-say reports, has burned almost to madness.

Professing a desire to reform politics and to promote the community's political morals, they furnish for their day and generation examples of a license in denunciatory speech, of a freedom in reckless personalities, and of a disposition for bigotry, uncharitableness and intolerance that may well cause the philosophic observer to pause and consider whether the process that evolves the highly developed type of man who, in his transcendental state of perfection becomes too good to remain in any political party, is a prodigious benefit to humanity or not.

CHAPTER XII.

A QUESTION OF STATE PRIDE AND PATRIOTISM.

THE desire of men to stand well before the eyes of the
world is among the first and strongest of the natural
instincts. A just pride of character is always respected
and when such pride includes likewise a due regard for
all things belonging to or connected with the person,
whether such things be worldly possessions, relatives,
friends or place of habitation, mankind will instantly
recognize one of the most stable and useful members of
the social order.

When the pride of the citizen in the matter of his place
of habitation, in his country and in its institutions, is
strongly developed men say he is patriotic; and whatever
his faults and failings may be his unselfish love of country
shines as the great redeeming quality of his nature.
Posterity will forgive his foibles if he is patriotic, and
history will know him only as an example for the sons
of the nation to emulate. That his patriotism has taught
him to guard and defend the good name of his country
or of his State may be assumed without question, as
otherwise he would not be possessed of the grand quality
which causes nations and governments to be remembered
and the names of men to be revered. In the length and
breadth of the American Union, where is the man to be
found who does not respect the feeling which we know
and define as " State pride." The pride of a people in

their State commands the respect and the admiration of persons residing outside its borders as it does those of people of foreign countries. We may be allowed to present several instances of the existence of the wholesome quality in American citizens by recalling recent noteworthy acts on the part of the people of Delaware—the first of the original thirteen colonies to enter the sisterhood of States. In the late celebration of the centennial of the adoption of the federal constitution, held in New York City, in which the Governors of the first thirteen colonies were the leading participants, it was proposed, without a suspicion or thought of opposition, that the representative of the State which is the largest center of population and wealth should head the column in the grand procession. To the surprise of everybody and to the amusement of some at first, the Governor of Delaware, the next smallest State in the Union, the Hon. B. T. Biggs, arose and in fit and proper address, having paid due honor to New York as the largest of the States in population and riches, reminded the assembled Governors of the precedence held by Delaware in the formation of the Union. The assertion of patriotism and proper State pride on the part of Governor Biggs had its effect and the State next to the smallest in territory of those in the Union was represented at the head of the line in the grand pageant of States as it moved before the eyes of the assembled millions in the American metropolis.

Again, it is a matter of recent knowledge that when an enterprising American, prompted by a speculative spirit,

sought to obtain possession of one of the ancient whip-
ping-posts of Delaware for the purpose of conducting a
profitable exhibition for the satisfaction of the morbid
curiosity of the prospectively assembled millions at the
coming World's Fair at Chicago, State pride and the
self-respect of the people arose at once and when the
morning came, succeeding a certain eventful night, the
whipping-post that was to have been held up before the
gaze of a vulgar world as Delaware's mode of punishing
her culprits, had been chopped into pieces, rendering it
necessary for the original-minded showman to abandon
the idea of obtaining possession of that particular "at-
traction."

It may be accepted as a safe assertion that citizens
possessed of so much patriotism and deep-rooted pride
as those of the State of the Bayards, the Biggses, the
Salisburys, the Greens, the Rosses, the Cochrans, the
Gilpins, the Higgins, the Comegys, the Masseys, the
Stockleys and the Naudains, would not permit an element
of its citizens, whether banded together as Reformers
in politics or as Independents issuing addresses to "the
voters of the State" against its public men, to import a
band of libelers and reckless defamers of its sons, regardless of the question of the political party to which they
belonged, and turn them loose like hungry jackals to
disgrace the State and the residents within its boundaries
by the miasma of their noisome trail and the unwhole-
some effects upon the peace of mind and self-respect
of a community of their unclean presence.

Between the State of Delaware and the State of Pennsylvania what a contrast is presented! The men who prate most about the " lost honor of Pennsylvania " are the men who disgrace and defame her. They who profess so much solicitude for her good name are the ones who furnished the material to the hostile press of a rival State to blacken her record and belittle her achievements before the eyes of her sister States.

When we reflect that the Pharisaic band which affects such high ground and such pure ideals in politics consists of the men who, in the formation of one of their recent " Reform Committees " adopted by a unanimous vote as one of their fundamental doctrines, a provision in their constitution against the introduction of electric cars in Philadelphia, the idea is apt to suggest itself that the community would perhaps hear without impatience any proposition contemplating the erection of a principality or of a State where they could form a government and live a life in accordance with their own ideas, unmolested by practical men and shunned by all who despise the libeller, the villifier and the exemplar of hypocricy and false pretense.

The citizens of Pennsylvania who are patriotic and who have a reasonable pride in their State, will perhaps be reluctant to agree with our Pharisaic mourners on the question of the alleged degeneracy of the State's power and importance. They will doubtless view the matter in the light of cold reason and common sense and see in the position of Pennsylvania to-day, one of the proudest eras she has ever enjoyed in her history ; will see her represented in the most important position in the National

Cabinet—the position which has dealings directly with the seventy million people of the land, the Postmaster Generalship—by a gentleman born and reared in the chief city of the State, and taken from the walks of busy mercantile life, the wisdom of whose appointment has been justified by the immense improvement and enlargement of the Postal Service under his practical and untiring hands. In the presence of the undoubted results of Postmaster General Wanamaker's work, the Pharisaic lamentations surely cannot receive encouragement. The honor of the State of Pennsylvania seems to be as bright in its possession of this shining member of the National Cabinet as it ever has been in its history.

The State has likewise the Second Comptroller of the Treasury, Colonel B. F. Gilkeson, who, it will perhaps be well to remind the weeping but defamatory Pharisees, amply maintains the honor of Pennsylvania at the National Capitol. Nor must it be forgotten that the State whose "honor" and "importance" have been so sadly obscured, has the satisfaction of seeing another of her sons in the responsible office of Commissioner of Customs, in Mr. Holliday, of Erie, a position which, perhaps, from a Pharisaic standpoint, does not count, since those composing the delectable band of libelers of their State would prefer to see all customs duties abolished and foreign goods admitted free in accordance with the doctrines of their real political apostle, Mr. Cleveland.

A consideration of the situation in connection with foreign missions, will also be likely to give the citizen

of Pennsylvania an idea or two about the satisfactory
condition of his State's honor that he will not acquire
by reading the Pharisaic pamphlet "against Quay
and Quayism " or the " address to voters of Pennsylvania." He will find one of the most important Courts of
Europe, that of St. Petersburg, effulgent with the presence
of a brilliant son of Pennsylvania, Mr. Charles Emory
Smith. His eyes may next wander to classic Greece
where they will observe another celebrated Pennsylva-
nian in the person of Colonel A. Loudon Snowden, who,
like Minister Smith, abundantly exemplifies the honor of
the State which the Pharisaic element among its citizens
takes such unaccountable pleasure in maligning.

The honor of Pennsylvania seems, in view of sub-
stantial facts, quite well maintained under the present
Republican administration, made possible by Senator
Quay and other able party leaders. The list of distinguished places occupied by its sons might be enlarged
were it worth the while. For example, mention might
be made of the fact that an eminent citizen of Philadelphia, Mr. James H. Windrim, graced the responsible
office of Supervising Architect of the Treasury Depart-
ment until he resigned the post to accept an important
appointment under the Mayor of Philadelphia, Mr.
Stuart.

These facts will doubtless impress themselves upon
" the voters of Pennsylvania " when the Pharisaic host
appeals to them to adopt their views and co-operate with
them in their work. It may be safely assumed also that

the honor of the State will find defenders, once the
defaming " Provisional Committee " sets about to broaden
the scope of its work and reveals itself to the country
voters in its true color, which should be unmistakable
black, emblematic of the aims of its calling against the
white record of the State and against the fame of its
public men.

CHAPTER XIII.

THE CROMWELLIAN ADJUNCT.

In one respect in particular the political Pharisee may be considered fortunate in the pursuit of his chosen work. While an earnest and practical world, absorbed in the business of working out its destiny, may be too much preoccupied to listen to his grievances as poured forth in doleful monotone in counting-room or sidewalk, on crowded thoroughfare, or as represented in soberly-worded circulars or pamphlets addressed to " the voters," he invariably has recourse to at least one sympathetic editor who will take up his case and make common cause with him against the common enemy.

If the editor himself is a person of witch-burning propensities, he is more than likely to be radical in his ideas, in his desires, and in his interpretation of the duties divinely imposed upon him and which constitute his " mission." He excels even the Pharisee himself in his zeal to take from Providence the work of punishing the unworthy and the wicked, lest the wrong-doer shall not feel the full extent of the penalty he deserves; and once he gets started in the witch-burning movement, the righteous anger and impatience of contradiction which burn in his heart are easily distinguishable in all his utterances, whether spoken or written, on the question of the hated object of his wrath. There is, in his self appointed undertaking to reform the evils of society and of politics, the suggestion of a resemblance to the harsh and austere Cromwell; and it is not unlikely that if he were given full rein we should be treated to the spectacle in this enlightened day and generation of some unceremonious beheading, the victims of which would be not kings of the blood royal, but eminent political leaders, who at present indulge in their comings and goings in undoubted security and safety to their property and persons.

As a type of the austere and thoroughly jaundiced Cromwellian reform editor, we may take an uncompromising promulgator of Pharisaic grievances and doctrines who has his abode and his newspaper establishment in Doylestown, Pennsylvania. The burden of his complaint through the spring and the summer, the autumn and the gray winter is United States Senator Quay. He is ferocious in his rage against this particular Republican leader, and the wonder is that the consuming passion of hate, which is supposed to be destructive in its effects on man's physical system, has not before this time made itself felt on the frame of the Doylestown Cromwell.

It is not improbable there is an intention on the part of this desperate editorial man to fight the hated Quay with his finger nails and perhaps also with his teeth, as the thoroughly aroused spirit of the " Protector,"—fresh from the inspiring experience of a meeting with our " best citizens " in the Philadelphia Board of Trade rooms, to devise means to overthrow the dreadful Quay,—whereat Mr. Editor found his importance enhanced by unusual attentions from those desirous of enlisting his services—

delivers the ultimatum through his newspaper which a cowering world may read with fear and trembling, thus:

"The Anti-Quay Republicans are in earnest in the purpose they have undertaken, and it may as well be understood they propose to fight Quay and Quayism with any and all weapons available—even to the extremity resorted to last year, the defeat of Republican legislative nominees who owe or tender fealty to Quay."

The imagination of the reader may roam over a vast field in its quest after all the instruments of torture which the witch-burning editor's fierce and boundless wrath makes permissible in his declaration of war against this particular Republican leader and member of the United States Senate; may wander from the editorial natural weapons previously suggested, which seem so much in keeping with the womanish, nervous tension of Sir Editor himself, to the devices of torture employed by the Spanish inquisition and may make choice of whatever the more or less blood-thirsty cravings of his nature shall elect, with assurance of the prompt approbation of this magnanimous editorial dispenser of human punishment.

It is possible that if Mr. Quay had taken time from his pursuit of National affairs, had dropped his somewhat responsible and trying task of electing a Republican President in 1888, abandoned his post as Chairman of the Republican National Committee for awhile, and betaken himself to Doylestown to pay his respects to Mr. Editor, the above proclamation of indiscriminate warfare against him "with any and all weapons available" would never have been written.   In the consideration of the question of what was wisest at the time the fact should be borne in mind that about six million voting people were directly interested in the result of the work which he had been selected to perform, and had he left "the party helm," even for such a short time as would have been necessary for him to take his visiting card to our dissatisfied Reform Editor in Doylestown, some of those six million might have raised protests and objections.   In such event there may be a reasonable doubt whether the supposed truant Chairman's explanation that he had "gone to Doylestown to keep from incurring the enmity of a certain Reform Editor" would have satisfied the clamorous legions in whose eyes the aforesaid editor would unquestionably appear as an object infinitesimally small in comparison with the importance of that political General, Quay, who led them to victory and whose stalwart figure is such a shining target for the Editorial Lilliputian's petty shafts at this time.

The reader will readily observe that even Reform Editors are fallible; that they have their ailments, their spells of indigestion, their attacks of jaundice, their over-wrought nerves.   If eminent, or prominent public men over-look them it is to be regretted, but at the same time it is doubtful if the unintentional failure to recognize their transcendent ability and superior worth justifies the formation of a movement or an organization, having in view the political destruction of those guilty of the crime of failing to render due homage to their importance as "moulders of public opinion." Those six million people who in 1888 went fairly mad with joy upon the announcement of the result of the Presidential election and paid due honors to the General who brought about the victory in their spontaneous vocal outburst

> "Quay! Quay!
> Won the Day!"

would hardly cast their decision, supposing them to be sitting as a jury on the trial of the grievances of our Cromwellian Doylestown Editor and his Pharisaic patrons, whether they be banded together as a "provisional committee" of dissatisfied tariff men, and dissatisfied stockholders in foreign insurance companies or not,—in favor of fighting the political Commander in question "with any and all weapons available."

Yet it would be obviously wrong for us to be harsh with the Doylestown Editor and his Pharisaic brethren on the "provisional committee" for their part against this noted Republican General. From the beginning of the world it has been customary for the strong, the vigorous and the lusty leaders of men to experience the effects of the jealousy, the envy, the malice and the general uncharitableness of the small-minded and petty ones. Incapable of rising to the height of the leaders whom they assail, incapable of performing acts which command the attention of their fellow-men and thus give them prominence, they wonder how it is that others have so much fame and celebrity while they are compelled to go through life unnoticed by the world. The

political General, Quay, whom our Pharisaic brethren
and their Doylestown Cromwellian adjunct are so vigor-
ously aiming their Lilliputian arrows at, is known throughout the length and breadth of a nation of nearly seventy
million souls as the Republican leader who managed to
a successful issue the campaign of his political party for
the Presidency in 1888. The Pharisees who have banded themselves together as his assailants, with their "provisional committee" are unknown beyond the confines
of the city of their habitation. They have their grievance
and their grudge against this party leader. The result
of his work has been to compel them to use the products
of the workingmen of their own country rather than the
fruits of the work of the laborers of Europe. If they
wish to continue to sell foreign-made goods to the
American public they must pay a higher import duty to
get it here. They do not desire to pay the higher duty,
and they do not wish to encourage the manufacture and
sale of American stockings, American woolens and
American fabrics. The cheap labor of the older world
enables them to buy the material lower there and sell it
higher in their own country.

"Gentlemen of the provisional committee for the defeat
of Quay and Quayism, is this not so?"

In the pursuit of the object of his hatred the political
Pharisee will not scruple, as we have heretofore shown,
to exaggerate all he may hear that is to the discredit of
the leader whom he and his band seek to overthrow.
Their ears are ever set to receive reports that defame
him, their tongues are ever ready to spread the hurtful

rumor, and their minds, like the poison that is wafted from the Upas tree, are ever prepared to shed upon the sunshine of fair belief and rational content of mind over every day experience, the shadow of culumny, suspicion and distrust and uncharitableness, and make men feel there is no good in anything of a political character, whether it be men or methods, save it shall come from the hands of Pharisees themselves, created to their liking and conveyed to the citizens after the form and style of the Pharisaic order.

Thus, reader, have we described, or attempted to describe, this singular element in our modern politics. If the mind of any one who shall have followed the description is led to reflect and to observe in his daily life more closely the traits of character of the persons who are the subject of this work, and the judgment on the question of their motives is thus rendered more clear, ample will have been the reward for the effort made and the aim which prompted the undertaking.